BAT CAN'T SLEEP
CARLY GLEDHILL
Macmillan Children's Books

Bat can't sleep.
She isn't like other bats.

They like to sleep during
the day. But Bat is too excited!

and JUMPS
all the way
through the
woods.

There's no stopping Bat.
She SWINGS through the trees.
Wheeee!

Then

SKATES

all the way

down the hill.

Bat is *still* not sleepy!

...Bat yawns.
Uh-oh...

Watch out, Bat!

PHEW!
Bat is caught,
just in time!

She **DIVES** into the water.

And **SWIMS** across the sea.

Bat **CLIMBS** up the hill.
She does feel a *little* bit
sleepy now . . .

What an exciting day!
At last, Bat . . .

...SLEEPS!
Sshh. Sweet dreams, Bat!

For Auntie Sue.
Sorry about all the spiders x – C.G.

First published 2021 by Macmillan Children's Books
an imprint of Pan Macmillan
The Smithson,
6 Briset Street,
London EC1M 5NR
EU representative: Macmillan Publishers Ireland Limited,
Mallard Lodge, Lansdowne Village, Dublin 4
Associated companies throughout the world

www.panmacmillan.com

ISBN: 978-1-5290-6061-4

1 3 5 7 9 8 6 4 2

A CIP catalogue record for this book is available from the British Library.

Printed in China

MIX
Paper from responsible sources
FSC® C116313
www.fsc.org